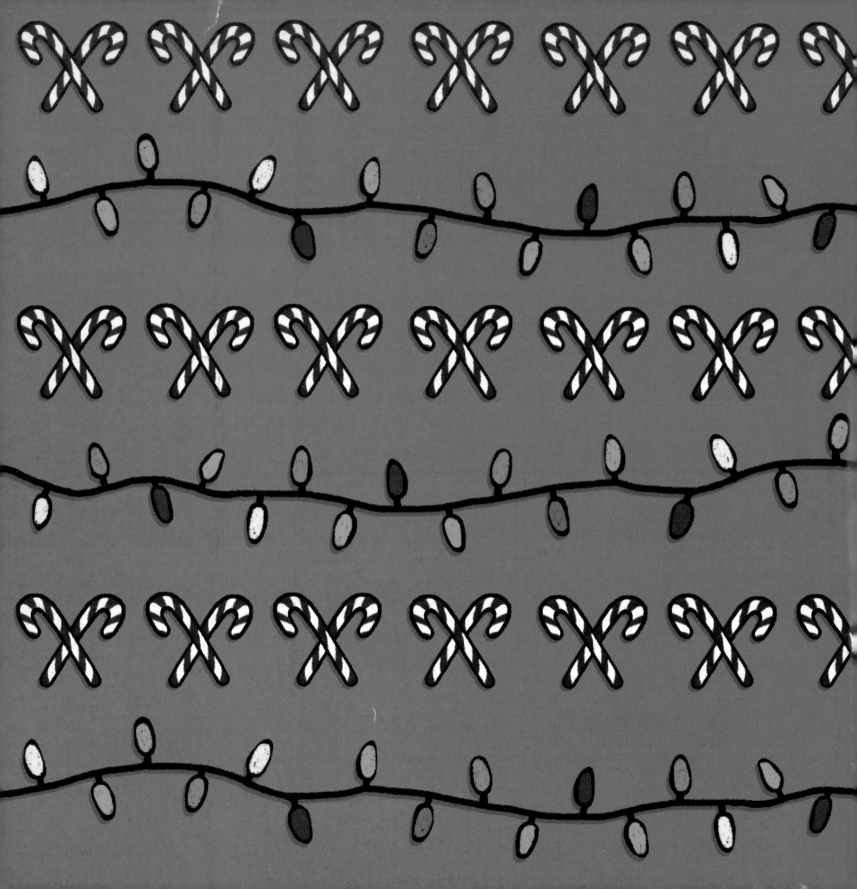

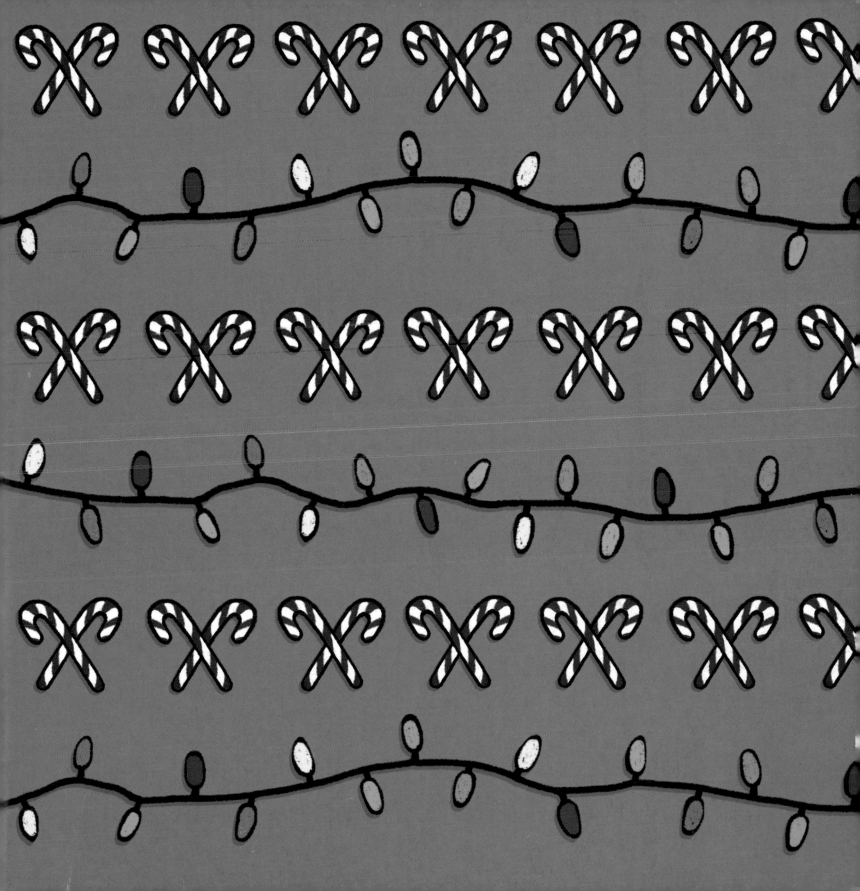

In memory of
Debbie Alvarez

Bloomsbury Publishing, London, Oxford, New York, New Delhi and Sydney

First published in the United States of America in 2016
by Bloomsbury Children's Books
1385 Broadway, New York, New York 10018

This edition first published in Great Britain in 2016 by Bloomsbury Publishing Plc
50 Bedford Square, London WC1B 3DP

Text and illustrations copyright © Salina Yoon 2016

The moral rights of the author/illustrator have been asserted

A CIP catalogue record for this book is available from the British Library

ISBN 978 1 4088 8256 6

Printed in China by Leo Paper Products, Heshan, Guangdong

1 3 5 7 9 10 8 6 4 2

www.bloomsbury.com

Penguin's Christmas Wish

Salina Yoon

BLOOMSBURY
LONDON OXFORD NEW YORK NEW DELHI SYDNEY

It was Christmas Eve. Pumpkin was getting ready for the best Christmas ever.
    "I wish we had a real Christmas tree," Pumpkin sighed.

Penguin knew there were no pine trees on the ice. But he had an idea.

Penguin packed the sled for a long journey.

Bootsy carried the ornaments,

Pumpkin held the star

and Grandpa took the presents.

Penguin led them away from their frozen home.

Deep in the heart of the forest,
a special friend was waiting.

Pinecone! My,
how you've grown!

The penguins decorated Pinecone with all the trimmings.

Now we're ready for Christmas!

"What a fine tree," said Grandpa.

WOW!

That night, the penguins
dreamed of Christmas wishes.

Penguin wanted to share Christmas with the whole forest. But there wasn't anyone else around.

While the penguins slept, a blizzard swept through the forest. The wind blew and blew.

On Christmas morning, the penguins returned. Not a single decoration hung from the tree.

"Christmas is not about decorations and presents," said Grandpa. "It is about being with the ones you love."

Penguin set off into the snow.

Penguin searched high and low. All
he could find were branches and twigs.

They were exactly
what he needed . . .

The penguins had a lovely day.

Grandpa and Penguin
caught Christmas dinner.

Bootsy knitted a
tree trunk cosy.

Rum-pa
pum-pum!

Pumpkin drummed
Christmas carols.

Everyone's Christmas
wish had come true . . .

. . . except for Penguin's.

Just then, the sun
warmed the air and
the snow began to melt.

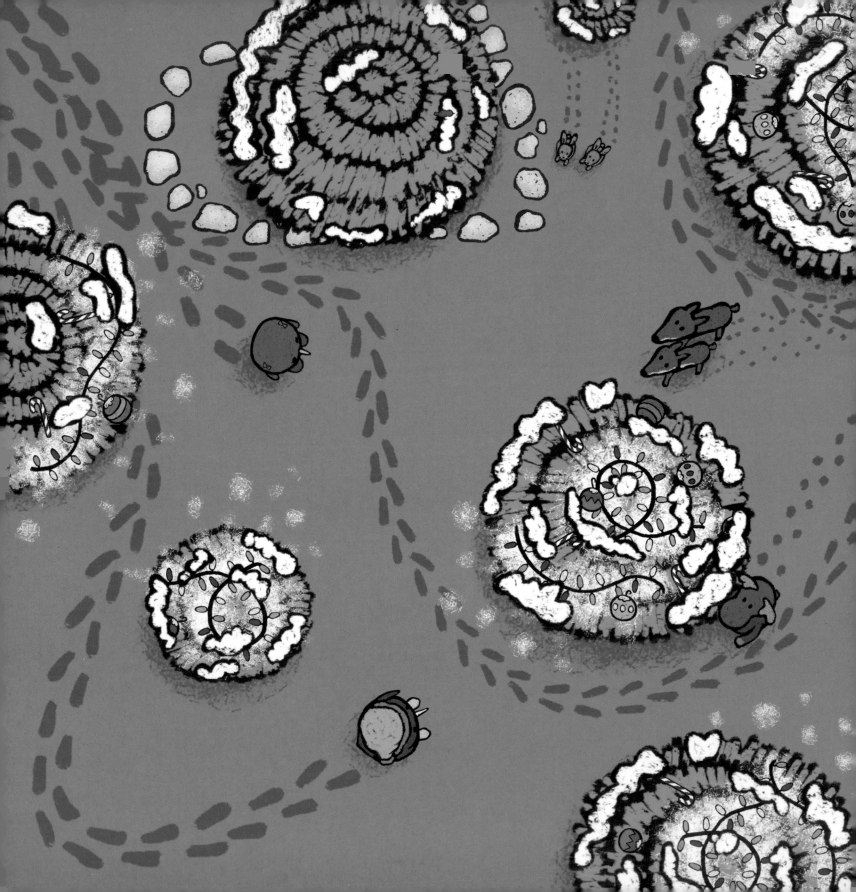

The storm had blown Pinecone's decorations on to every tree. And the magic of Christmas lit up the forest!

Friends both old and new
gathered from far and wide.
Penguin's Christmas wish had
come true!

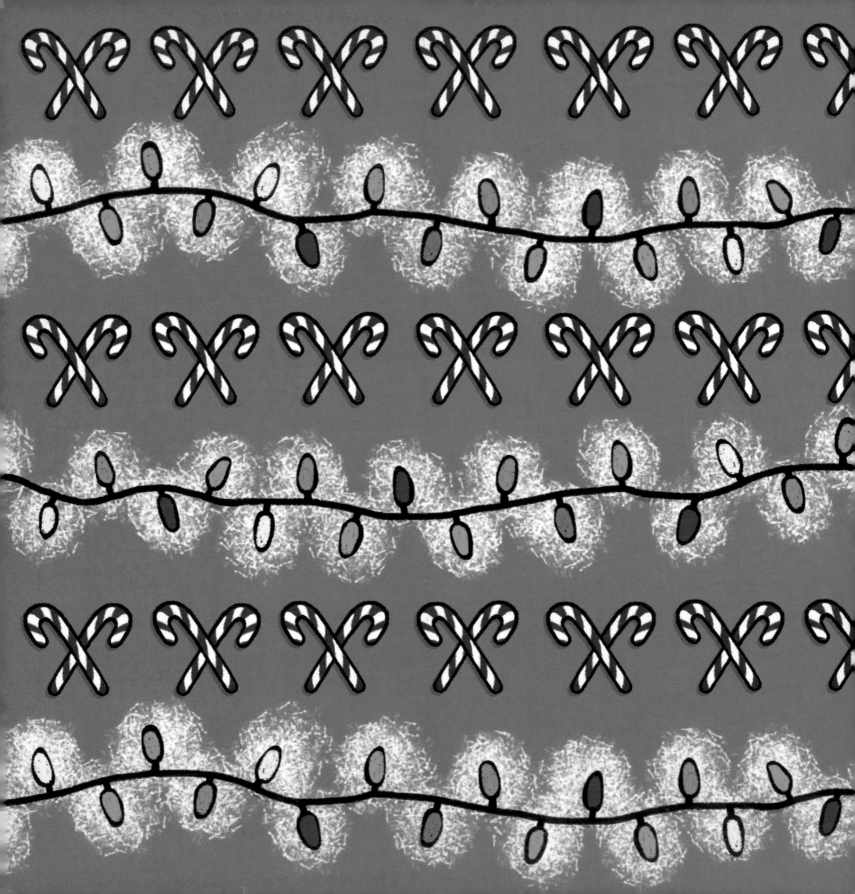

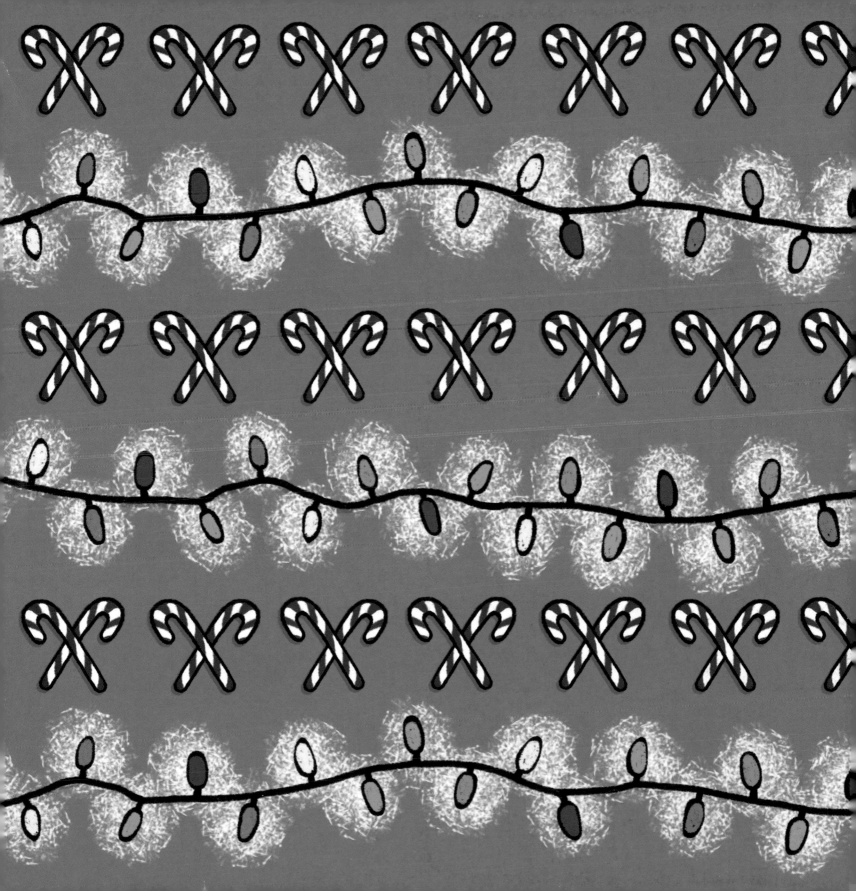